o + Lea

by **Monica Wesolowska**

illustrated by **Kenard Pak**

scholastic press / new york

Leo.

Counting.

Two
trees.

Three
noisy squirrels.

Five
big steps
into
school.

Eight
new classmates
shout, “Hello!”
Leo smiles
back.

Thirteen
raindrops tap
the window
one autumn afternoon,
and Leo counts
them all.

Twenty-one
words dance
across the page.
Leo usually likes to
count the words aloud.
"Leo," his teacher says,
"count softly, please."

Thirty-four
snowflakes
silently drift down
the winter morning
a new girl arrives.
"Leo, meet Lea,"
his teacher says.
Leo is quiet,
but when Lea smiles,
he leans closer to see
what she is doing.

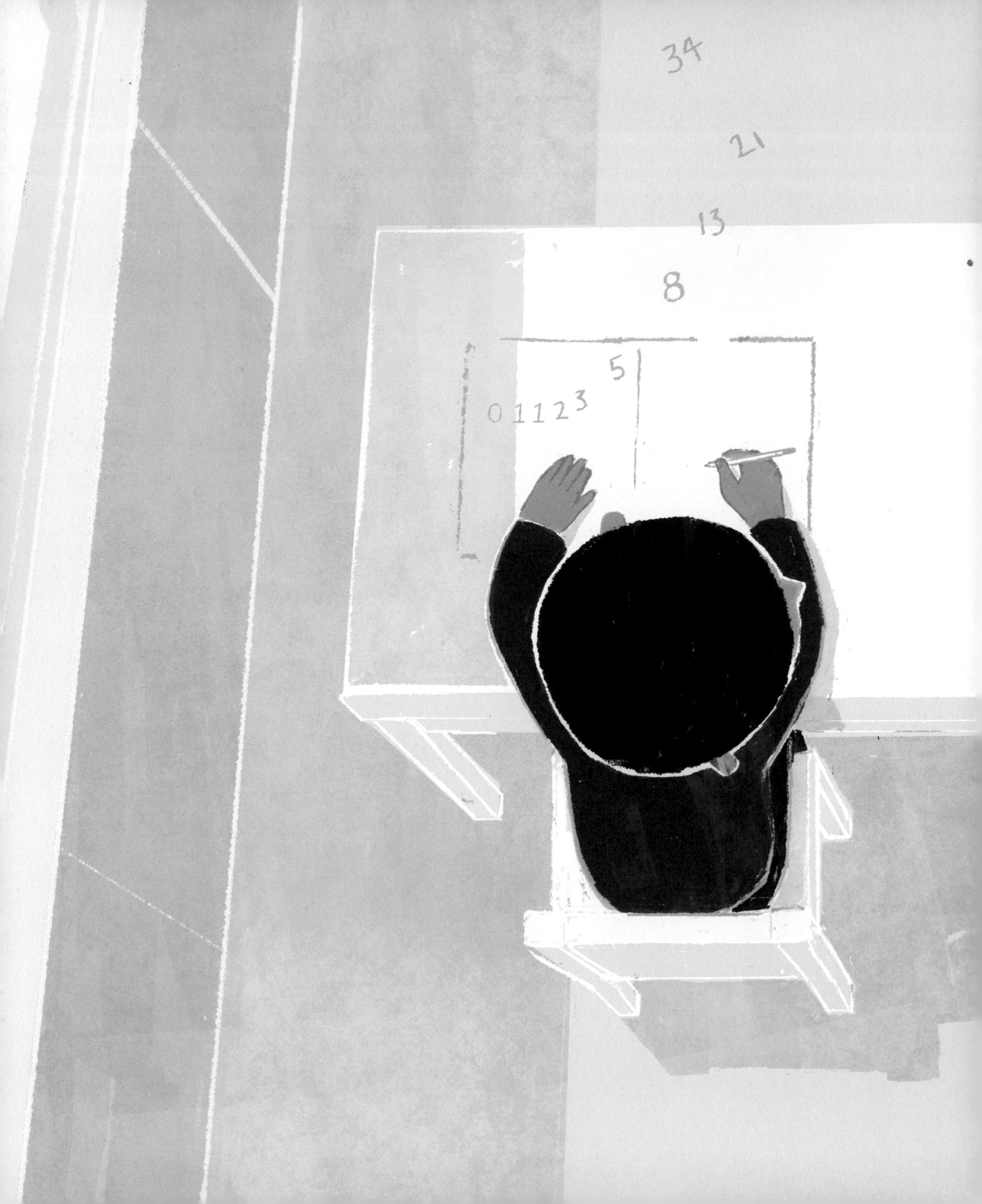

34

21

13

8

5

0 1 1 2 3

FINISH

Fifty-five
daisies pop up
in spring,
and Leo wants
to count them.
But the playground feels
too big and hard.
Balls bounce,
hands clap,
children cheer.
As squawking birds
fill the sky,
Leo's numbers
jumble in his mind.
And so he plugs his ears
and tells his teacher
he is going to find
some peace.

Thirty-four
stepping stones
make a path.
As recess ends,
Leo's classmates leave
their noisy games
and join their teacher.
Counting stones, they reach
the schoolyard garden
just in time to hear
a happy shout.

"Twenty-one leaves!" Leo exclaims. "Lea, I see a pattern!" Lea beams and tells everyone, "I love patterns. Want to see more?"

Thirteen
blossoms
burst from
the page.
Galaxies of
petals spiral
up and up.

Eight
chattering classmates
gather petals
to take inside.

Five
fingers
link
each hand.

Three
quick spins.

Two
friends.

Counting.

Skyward.

MATH CONNECTS US ALL A Few Words on Fibonacci and Friendship

FROM THE AUTHOR

Thanks to a child who told me he liked math more than stories, I set out to write this story based on a math pattern, the Fibonacci sequence. This sequence is simple to start. Beginning with 0 and 1, you reach each subsequent number by adding the previous two. For example: 0+1=1. From there, 1+1=2, and 1+2=3, and 2+3=5. Although the Fibonacci sequence increases forever, the words on each page of this book increase like this: 1, 1, 2, 3, 5, 8, 13, 21, 34, 55, before reversing and returning to 1.

The first known use of this sequence was in Sanskrit poetry over two thousand years ago. Indian scholars had already studied it for centuries when the medieval mathematician Leonardo of Pisa, later known as Fibonacci, described it in a book teaching people to use Hindu Arabic numerals. Leonardo himself may not have recognized the significance of this pattern named after him, but later scholars noticed something astonishing about it. The Fibonacci sequence appears throughout nature. For example, did you notice that the apple blossoms in this book have five petals? As it happens, flowers often have a Fibonacci number of petals. Fibonacci numbers also appear in the spiraling arrangement of many leaves and seeds. Beyond its relationship to the way some plants grow, this sequence has many other intriguing properties. For example, the ratios of successive Fibonacci numbers approach an irrational number that starts with 1.618 and goes on forever. This irrational number, known as Phi, is celebrated as the "golden ratio." For all these reasons and more, it's not just mathematicians who continue to study this sequence to this day.

For me, the Fibonacci sequence seemed a natural framework for growing a story about two children and their budding friendship. Their story reminded me of myself as a child, alone on the playground, making up stories and wondering how to find a friend. Just as Leo counts alone until he connects with Lea, I counted each word of this book by myself until my story connected with an illustrator who made it bloom with his own Fibonacci-inspired art. Thanks to a child who liked math more than stories, I realized math connects us all. And now, I hope this story connects with you.

—Monica Wesolowska

FROM THE ARTIST

The art in this book is inspired by Fibonacci color hexadecimal code sequences, a subtle visual clue to how Leo views the world. A hexadecimal code, or hex code, is a number given to a color on the computer, which allows everyone who works digitally to share the same exact colors. I used hex codes that, when arranged in a group, match the Fibonacci sequence. One group, or sequence, goes from turquoise to minty greens to a strong yellow. My favorite sequence, which appears a lot in the book, transitions from dark purples to mauve and then to hot pinks. As the book progresses, and the story builds toward the climax, the colors become more intense. I also used a lot of line work to convey Lea's love for drawing. While almost all the artwork was done on the computer, I worked with traditional pencils and gouache washes to create Lea's drawings, her flowering creativity, and, finally, the big imagination she shares with Leo. I hope readers can learn about different ways of experiencing the world, and know there's always someone who can share these experiences with you.

—Kenard Pak

**For Ben L., who was tired of books about dinosaurs;
and for David, Miles, and Ivan, of course! —M.W.**

For Suna Ray —K.P.

Thank you to Keith Devlin, Arthur Ogus, and Leslie Badoian for vetting the mathematical information found in the author's note.

Thank you to Lyn Miller-Lachmann for her insightful feedback on the representation of neurodiversity in the story.

 Published by Scholastic Press, an imprint of Scholastic Inc., *Publishers since 1920.* SCHOLASTIC, SCHOLASTIC PRESS, and associated logos are trademarks and/or registered trademarks of Scholastic Inc. • Library of Congress Cataloging-in-Publication Data available • ISBN 978-1-338-30287-5
10 9 8 7 6 5 4 3 2 1 22 23 24 25 26 • Printed in China 62 • First edition, August 2022 • Kenard Pak's artwork was created using pencil, gouache, watercolor, and digital mediums. The text type was set in Helvetica Neue Medium and display type was set in Skia Bold and Skia Black. • The book was printed and bound at RR Donnelley Asia. • Production was overseen by Catherine Weening. • Manufacturing was supervised by Shannon Rice. • The book was art directed and designed by Marijka Kostiw and edited by Tracy Mack.